The cre8ors of the *New York Times* bestseller *Duck! Rabbit!* are up to their old tricks again!

> I know! Let's make a book about words.

> No, let's make a book about numbers.

> Words.

> Numbers.

> Words!

> Numbers!

> Words!!

> Numbers!!

What do you get when you combine a word and a number? A wumber!
Paying tribute to William Steig's *C D B!*, book cre8ors Amy Krouse Rosenthal
and Tom Lichtenheld have wri10 and illustr8ed this s2pendous book
that is perfect 4 readers in kindergar10 and up.

## PRAISE FOR *WUMBERS*

> Let's 4ge ahead!

"Playful." —*The Wall Street Journal*

"This book can be the center of family fun." —*Chicago Tribune*

"An inspired picture book that encourages cre8tive wordplay." —*School Library Journal*

"A true testament to phonological awareness . . . likely to intrigue and stimulate." —*Kirkus Reviews*

"Successful. . . . Entertainingly complex." —*Publishers Weekly*

"A bounty of new, clever shortcuts. . . . Pure fun, from 1 to 80. . . . A playful way
to describe scenes and situations." —*Shelf Awareness for Readers*

"This book will get you thinking and giggling." —*Children's Literature*

A Junior Library Guild Selection
A Parents' Choice Awards Recommended Seal

Have you read *Alice in 1derland?*

Are you usually prompt, or do you 10d 2 be l8 and keep others w8ing?

What do you think you'll be like as 18ager?

What question would you ask a 4tune teller?

This is kind of in10se, but do you think outer space goes on 4ever or do you think it 7tually got to end somewhere?

What is the lati2ude and longi2ude of where you live?

Do you know what the path is 2 true enligh10ment?

Have you ever tiptoed through the 2lips?

WRI10 BY AMY KROUSE ROSENTHAL

ILLUSTR8ED BY TOM LICHTENHELD

chronicle books · san francisco

Oh, and I just love your **2-2.**

They are pre**10**ding.

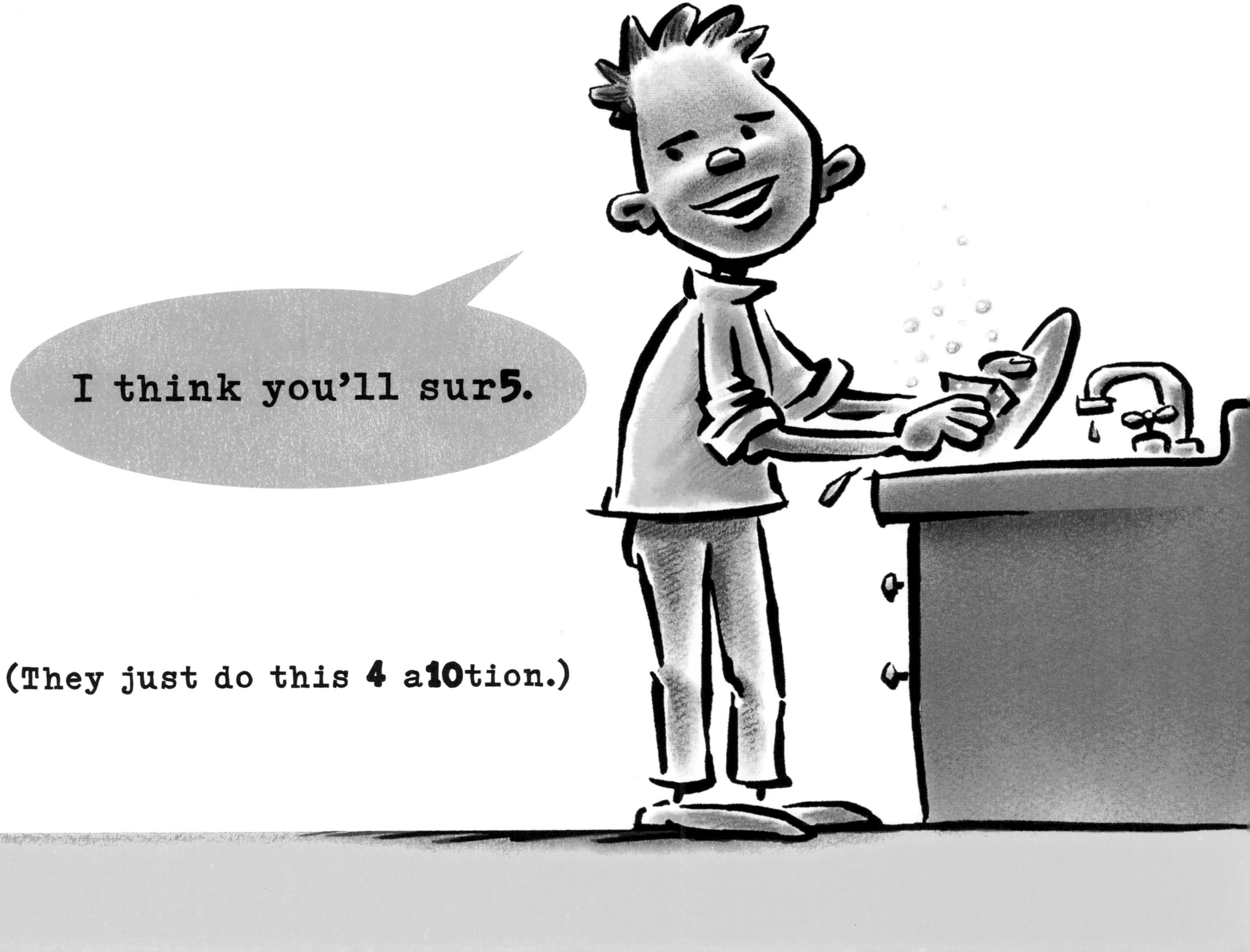


(They just do this 4 a10tion.)

Those sure are some orn8 10tacles.

Wheeeeeeeee! Flying 10ies!

He lost his first **2**th!
He is el**8**ed!

When you m8 4ever,

They are in a **4**eign country.
Their **2r** guide is transl**8**ing.

C'est **4**midable, non?

It's gr**8**, right?

Pure con**10**tment.

A sh**80** spot **4** reading and writing.

We dedic**8** this book **2**
William Steig, the cre**8**or of *C D B!*
(cer**10**ly the inspiration
for this book) and so many
other cla**6**. —A.K.R. & T.L.

First Chronicle Books LLC paperback edition, published in 2015.
Originally published in hardcover in 2012 by Chronicle Books LLC.

Text © 2012 by Amy Krouse Rosenthal. Illustrations © 2012 by Tom Lichtenheld.

ISBN 978-1-4521-4122-0

The Library of Congress has cataloged the previous edition under ISBN 978-1-4521-1022-6.

Manufactured in China.

Book design by Sara Gillingham. Typeset in ClickClack and Ultinoid.
The illustrations in this book were created with ink and PanPastels.

10 9 8 7 6 5 4 3 2 1

Chronicle Books LLC
680 Second Street
San Francisco, California 94107

www.chroniclekids.com

Have you read Alice in 1derland?

Are you usually prompt, or do you 10d 2 be l8 and keep others w8ing?

What do you think you'll be like as 18ager?

What question would you ask a 4tune teller?

This is kind of in10se, but do you think outer space goes on 4ever or do you think it 7tually got to end somewhere?

What is the lati2ude and longi2ude of where you live?

Do you know what the path is 2 true enligh10ment?

Have you ever tiptoed through the 2lips?

AMY spends her exis10ce writing books, making films, and 10ding to her family.
Visit her in the st8 of Illinois and at www.whoisamy.com.

TOM lives in Illinois, 2. The last 1 to his website is a ro10 egg.
www.tomlichtenheld.com

## ALSO BY AMY KROUSE ROSENTHAL AND TOM LICHTENHELD

### *Duck! Rabbit!*

"Funny by any standard."
—*The New York Times* Book Review

★ "Duck? Rabbit? As kids will readily see, it depends on how you look at it."
—*Publishers Weekly*, starred review

★ ". . . [a] modern twist on a classic form."
—*Kirkus Reviews*, starred review

★ "How cute is this? Really, really cute."
—*Booklist*, starred review

A *New York Times* Bestseller
A Parents' Choice Awards Silver Honor
A Time Magazine's Top 10 Children's Books of the Year